For Todd, with love —S.L.-J.

For Vanessa, meine Maus —A.B.

Text copyright © 2014 by Sally Lloyd-Jones

Cover art and interior illustrations copyright © 2014 by Alexandra Boiger

Visit us on the Web! randomhouse.com/kids

Educators and librarians, for a variety of teaching tools, visit us at RHTeachersLibrarians.com

*Library of Congress Cataloging-in-Publication Data*

Lloyd-Jones, Sally.

Poor Doreen : a fishy tale / by Sally Lloyd-Jones ; illustrated by Alexandra Boiger.—First edition.

pages cm

Summary: A fish named Doreen gets into all sorts of trouble on the way to see her cousin.

ISBN 978-0-375-86918-1 (trade) — ISBN 978-0-375-96918-8 (glb) — ISBN 978-0-375-98786-1 (ebook)

[1. Fishes—Fiction.] I. Boiger, Alexandra, illustrator. II. Title.

PZ7.L77878Po 2013

[E]—dc22

2012047195

The text of this book is set in ITC Goudy Sans.

The illustrations were rendered in watercolor, gouache, pencil, and colored pencil on Fabriano watercolor paper.

Book design by Rachael Cole

MANUFACTURED IN CHINA

10 8 6 4 2 1 3 5 7 9

First Edition

# POOR DOREEN

## A Fishy Tale

written by Sally Lloyd-Jones  illustrated by Alexandra Boiger

schwartz & wade books · new york

In the deep drowsy waters

of a long winding creek,

an Ample Roundy Fish called Miss Doreen Randolph-Potts

is swimming along,

on her way upstream

to visit her second cousin twice removed

who's just had 157 babies. . . .

But.
Oh dear.

By the water's edge
a Fisherman wearing a coat the color of the sun
and a Great Blue Heron wearing a coat the color of a stormy sky
with a neck like an S
for SPEAR
are fishing.

(Oh, poor Doreen. Yes.)

Doreen doesn't see them.

Through the glittering water

she spies only a dragonfly,

darting,

dancing deliciously above her.

"GOODY!"

Doreen cries,

"How lucky for me!

A lovely snack for my journey!"

and glides to the surface,
her mouth gurgling out into a big round O
for OPEN.

In one giant GULP,

Doreen swallows the dragonfly whole.

Oh.

But.

Except.

Wait.

It's not a dragonfly.
Oh, poor Doreen. No.
It's a HOOK.
And it's not a treat.
It's a TRAP.
And the one thing you're not is lucky.
This may be the most awful day of your life.
Worse—it may be your . . .
LAST.

The Fisherman arches his back into a
C for CATCH!

The Great Blue Heron braces
for his dinner.
(Oh dear.)

The end of the line that holds the hook
that holds the dragonfly
that holds Doreen
speeds through the water
closer and closer to
the Fisherman wearing a coat the color of the sun
and the Great Blue Heron wearing a coat the color of a stormy sky.

"WHEE!" cheers Doreen. "What a REMARKABLE swimmer I am!"

I'll be with my cousin in no time!"

The Fisherman jerks the line, raises his fishing pole
high and back,
gives one final pull and . . .

"YIPPEE!" cries Doreen. "I'm going on an outing!"

Oh dear, Doreen. No.
You're not.

You're going out and up and down

And now you're doing a
BIG BELLY-FISH-FLOP

at the feet of a Fisherman wearing a coat the color of the sun
and a Great Blue Heron wearing a coat the color of a stormy sky.

The skillful Fisherman carefully removes the hook.

"How DELIGHTFUL!"

gasps the poor foolish fish.

"A little rest on my journey!"

Oh, poor Doreen. No.
It's not a rest.
It's THE END!

No sooner is the hook out than
the Great Blue Heron launches from
his lookout,

exploding into the air,
unfolding his wings
        into a great flapping W
        for . . .
WATCH OUT!

Yes, WATCH OUT, Doreen!
        You're about to be . . .

        EATEN!

From under the Fisherman's very nose,
the Great Blue Heron SNAPS the fish up
and SWOOPS off into the shallows.

He struts about on those long stick legs,
holds his head high in the air,
yes, and puffs his chest out
into a great big P
for PROUD.

And with a mouthful of Ample Roundy Fish, he takes off.

"BRAVO! Thank you, kind sir!" cheers the unfortunate Doreen.

"How considerate.

To escort me on my journey upstream!"

The Great Blue Heron has never had
a fish dinner thank him before.

"And, sir?" Doreen asks him.

"Are you, by any chance"—
what made her ask this we shall never know—
"an EGRET?"

Oh, help!

Poor Doreen.

Asking a Great Heron if he is an Egret is as bad as asking your teacher,

"Are you, by any chance, related to a Poisonous Toad?"

When the fish-eating machine hears Doreen's ignorant question,
he has to set her straight,
has to open his beak to snap—

"Good gracious, madam!

I am NO SUCH THING!"

In that instant
Doreen slips from his jaws—

plunging

and plummeting

and twisting

and turning

and—

"Look!!" she cries.

"I'm FLYING!"
Oh, poor Doreen. No.
Not Flying.
FALLING.

"WHOOPEE!" she shouts.
"I didn't know I could FLY!"

Oh dear, Doreen. No.
You really CAN'T.

Swimming through the sky . . . .

. . . and into the glittering water,
the fish falls.

Far from
the Fisherman wearing a coat the color of the sun
and the Great Blue Heron wearing a coat the color of a stormy sky.

Back into the deep drowsy water, at last,

curving

arching

weaving

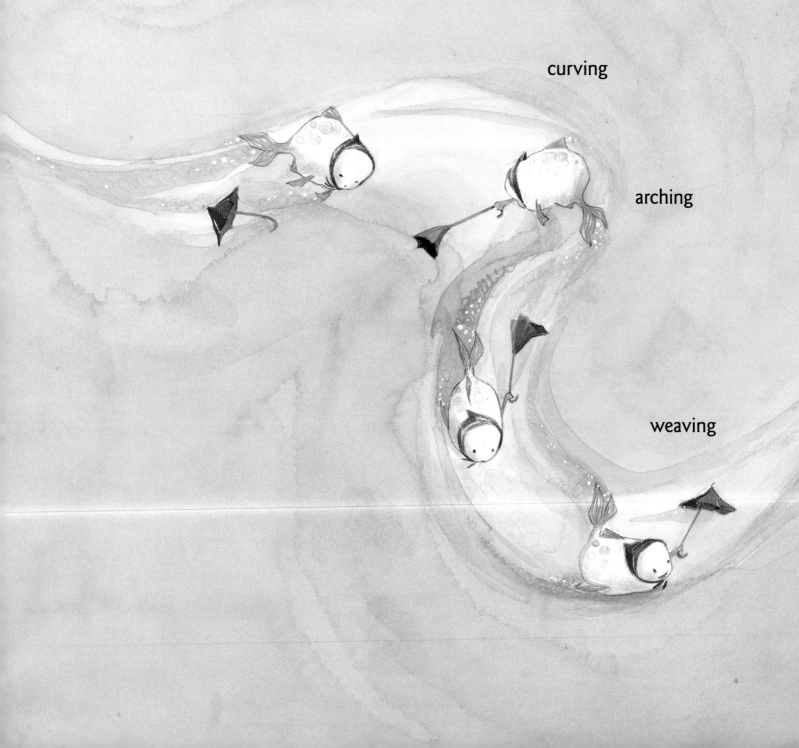

in a beautiful S
for SWIMMING.

upstream

rushing

"WONDERFUL!" she cries.

"What a PLEASANT journey I've had!"

The surface of the water grows smooth once more.

The Great Blue Heron flies off so no one can see him blushing.

And so it was that a Fisherman lost his catch
and a Great Blue Heron lost his dinner
and his pride.

And a little girl heading out with her fishing net saw only her daddy heading home wearing a coat the color of the sun.

And no sign at all of a Great Blue Heron wearing a coat the color of a stormy sky.

Or an extremely rare Southern Belle Ample Roundy Fish called Miss Doreen Randolph-Potts.

(Who was at that very moment having a marvelous reunion with her second cousin twice removed and her 157 babies and telling them the most incredible high-flying fishy tale no one would ever have believed in a million years—if it weren't true.)